This Little Tiger book
belongs to:

_____

_____

_____

For Mark, James, Joe and Jess ~ JH
For Matilda Rose, with love ~ VB

LITTLE TIGER PRESS

An imprint of Magi Publications

1 The Coda Centre, 189 Munster Road, London SW6 6AW

www.littletigerpress.com

First published in Great Britain 2009

This edition published 2010

Text copyright © Julia Hubery 2009

Illustrations copyright © Victoria Ball 2009

Julia Hubery and Victoria Ball have asserted their rights
to be identified as the author and illustrator of this work under the
Copyright, Designs and Patents Act, 1988

A CIP catalogue record for this book is available
from the British Library

All rights reserved • ISBN 978-1-84506-970-4

LTP/1800/0035/0610

Printed in China

2 4 6 8 10 9 7 5 3 1

Christmas
With You

Julia Hubery

illustrated by
Victoria Ball

LITTLE TIGER PRESS
London

Wide awake when the world is still,

watch the snow fall, soft and slow.

Tiptoe down
to catch
the **thrill,**
our faces
lit by
candle glow.

Eager eyes are shining bright
as papers **crackle**,
ribbons curl.

Find a shimmering world of white –

swoop and dip and dance and whirl!

Catch a **snowflake** on your nose,

make an **angel**,

make a **friend**.

Run and toast our **tingling** toes,

wish today would **never** end!

Luscious,
scrumptious,
richly sumptuous,

fun and feasting all together.

Playing games with clues that send us

racing for the
hidden treasure.

Fly on wings of ice, so daring,

till we tumble in surprise!

Voices bright, with lanterns flaring –

sing out under crystal skies!

After all the celebrating,

up the stairs we softly tread . . .

There we'll find a warm bed waiting,
there we'll lay your sleepy head.

So close your eyes, and drift away

in tender dreams
of Christmas Day.

Share in the joy of Christmas

with these Little Tiger Press books . . .

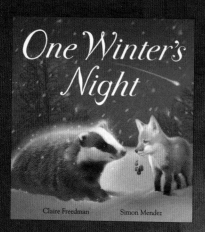

One Winter's Night
Claire Freedman · Simon Mendez

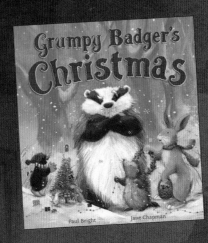

Grumpy Badger's Christmas
Paul Bright · Jane Chapman

The Best Christmas Ever!
Marni McGee · Gavin Scott

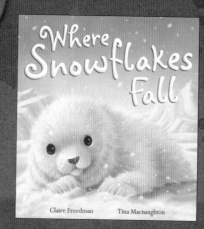

Where Snowflakes Fall
Claire Freedman · Tina Macnaughton

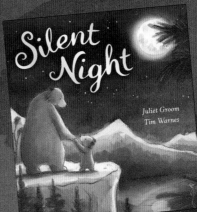

Silent Night
Juliet Groom · Tim Warnes

The First Snow
M Christina Butler · Frank Endersby

For information regarding any of the above titles or for our catalogue, please contact us:

Little Tiger Press, 1 The Coda Centre,
189 Munster Road, London SW6 6AW
Tel: 020 7385 6333 Fax: 020 7385 7333
E-mail: info@littletiger.co.uk
www.littletigerpress.com